# Disney PRINCESS

# Spring Sunshine

## PaRragon

Bath • New York • Cologne • Melbourne • Delhi
Hong Kong • Shenzhen • Singapore

18  1
14  15      3
13          16      2  5
12              17  4
11              6
10          7
9      8

2

Belle and the Beast are enjoying a spring dance outside. Connect the dots in the sky to see the different cloud shapes.

Good work!
Add a reward
sticker.

Answers on page 32

Merida has lost her basket of flowers.
Help her find it by following the right path.

A

B

C

Good work!
Add a reward
sticker.

4

Answer on page 32

Only two of these pictures are exactly the same. Can you spot them?

A

B

C

D

E

Did you find the matching pictures?

Add a reward sticker.

Answer on page 32

*Chirp, chirp!*
Belle and Chip say
hello to the baby birds.
How many birds do
you see on this page?

Add
a reward
sticker.

**6**

Answer on page 32

I can see          birds.

Draw a line to match each princess with her special friend.

Are the princesses with their friends now?

Answers on page 32

1

2

3

4

5

A

B

C

D

E

Taking turns with a friend, draw one line between two dots. When you complete a box, write your initial in the box and give yourself one point. Give yourself two points if the box contains a flower. Whoever has more points at the end of the game wins and gets a reward sticker.

Add a reward sticker.

Everyone is excited about spring. Use the key
to color the basket of eggs.

1 = Yellow

2 = Blue

3 = Green

4 = Orange

5 = Red

6 = Purple

Add
a reward
sticker.

9

Cinderella is dancing at the spring ball.
Can you find five differences between the two pictures below?

Have you found
all five differences?

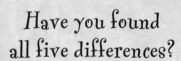

Add
a reward
sticker.

Answers on page 32

It's a beautiful spring day. Draw a rainbow for Aurora,
then color in the picture.

How many eggs can
you see in the basket?

I can see

eggs.

Add
a reward
sticker.

Snow White's animal friends are playing hide-and-seek!

Can you help Snow White find her friends? Put a check mark under each one you find.

Good work! Add a reward sticker.

**13**

Answers on page 32

Can you find "flower" four times in the grid below? Color a flower shape as you find each word.

F L O W E R F F
N R A T U C L
J E P N F A O
T W L E Y L W
P O T U N I E
F L B M J L R
U F L O W E R

Add a reward sticker.

Help the little animals create a spring dress for Cinderella.

Add a reward sticker.

Trace the picture to see what
Rapunzel is painting.

Rapunzel is
painting a

_____.

Add
a reward
sticker.

# Reward
# Stickers

© Disney

Just
for Fun!

Can you help Jasmine find her way to the spring flowers?

Add a reward sticker.

Answer on page 32

Flounder wants to play! Guide him through
the maze to Ariel.

Add
a reward
sticker.

Start here

Answer on page 32

Tiana has baked some yummy cupcakes.
Help her finish them by decorating them.

How many pink
flowers can you count
on this page?

I can see

pink flowers.

Add
a reward
sticker.

Answer on page 32

Snow White and some of the dwarfs want to play tic-tac-toe!
Choose between a heart and star shape and play along with a friend.

Add
a reward
sticker.

Princess Aurora goes for a ride on a spring day. Color in this picture, then give yourself a reward sticker.

Add
a reward
sticker.

Rapunzel is painting some eggs. Help her complete the flower pattern designs on the egg below by drawing in the flower that comes next in each row.

Add a reward sticker.

Answers on page 32

Replace each letter with the one that comes after it in the alphabet to find out what this bunny is thinking.

I _____ you.
K N U D

Add
a reward
sticker.

Answer on page 32

Tiana and her friends are getting ready for a big event! Write the first letter of each character's name on the blanks to find out what the event is.

## The Spring

_____ _____ _____ _____ _____ _____

Good work! Add a reward sticker.

**25**

Answer on page 32

Rapunzel wants to celebrate springtime. Help her by decorating her hair with some pretty flowers, then color her in.

Add a reward sticker.

# Trace the picture to see what Princess Ariel wants to decorate.

Good work!
Add a reward
sticker.

Answer on page 32

Merida is on a spring walk. Can you spot five differences between these two pictures?

Color a flower below for each difference you find.

Add a reward sticker.

**28**

Answers on page 32

Rapunzel is so excited that it's spring. Using the grid, copy the picture on the right and then color her in.

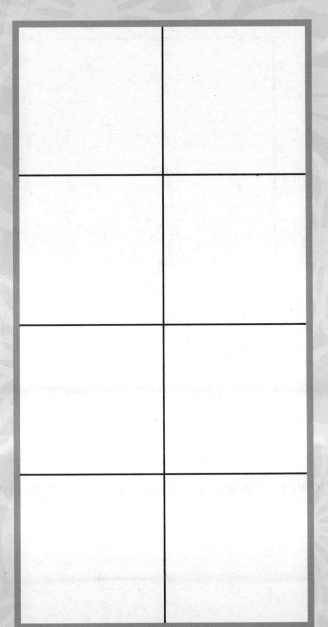

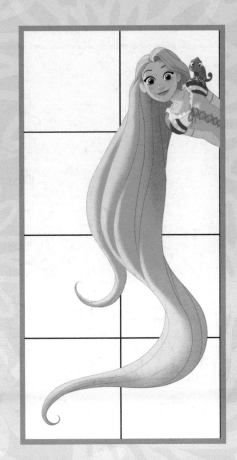

These rabbits are playing hide-and-seek. Can you find four differences between the two pictures?

Color a flower below for each difference you find.

Add
a reward
sticker.

Belle loves talking to the birds. Find and circle the shadow that matches this picture of Belle and her bird friends.

a

b

c

d

Answer on page 32

Add a reward sticker.

# Answers

**Pages 2–3:**
The connected dots show clouds in the shape of a bird, a heart, and a flower.

**P. 4:** Path A leads to the basket of flowers.

**P. 5:** C and D are exactly the same.

**P. 6:** There are 6 birds on the page.

**P. 7:**
1–C  2–D
3–B  4–A
5–E

**P. 10:**

**P. 11:**
There are
7 eggs.

**Pages 12 - 13:**

**P. 14:**

| F | L | O | W | E | R | F |
|---|---|---|---|---|---|---|
| N | R | A | T | U | C | L |
| J | E | P | N | F | A | O |
| T | W | L | E | Y | L | W |
| P | O | T | U | N | I | E |
| F | L | B | M | J | L | R |
| U | F | L | O | W | E | R |

**P. 16:** Rapunzel is painting a butterfly.

**P. 17:**

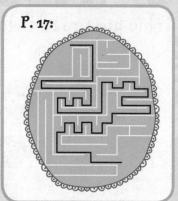

**P. 18:**

**P. 19:**
There are 6 pink flowers.

**P. 22:**
Row 1: Yellow flower,
Row 2: Green flower,
Row 3: Pink flower.

**P. 23:** The puzzle spells: I love you.

**P. 25:** The Spring Parade

**P. 27:** Ariel wants to decorate a seashell.

**P. 28:**

**P. 29:**

**P. 31:** C

32